For Rodrigo Ortega, a little knight
with a big heart.
— GILLES TIBO

For Maxime, Loïc and Florent.
— GENEVIÈVE DESPRÉS

The Little Knight Who Battled Monsters

GILLES TIBO
GENEVIÈVE DESPRÉS

Scholastic Canada Ltd.
Toronto New York London Auckland Sydney
Mexico City New Delhi Hong Kong Buenos Aires

Scholastic Canada Ltd.
604 King Street West, Toronto, Ontario M5V 1E1, Canada

Scholastic Inc.
557 Broadway, New York, NY 10012, USA

Scholastic Australia Pty Limited
PO Box 579, Gosford, NSW 2250, Australia

Scholastic New Zealand Limited
Private Bag 94407, Botany, Manukau 2163, New Zealand

Scholastic Children's Books
Euston House, 24 Eversholt Street, London NW1 1DB, UK

www.scholastic.ca

Library and Archives Canada Cataloguing in Publication
Tibo, Gilles, 1951-
[Petit chevalier qui combattait les monstres. English]
The little knight who battled monsters / Gilles Tibo ; illustrated by Geneviève Després ;
translated by Petra Johannson.
(The little knight)
Translation of: Le petit chevalier qui combattait les monstres.
ISBN 978-1-4431-3384-5
I. Després, Geneviève, illustrator II. Johannson, Petra, translator
III. Title. IV. Titre: Petit chevalier qui combattait les monstres. English
PS8589.I26P42613 2015   jC843'.54   C2015-901871-4

6 5 4 3 2 1   Printed in Canada   119   15 16 17 18 19

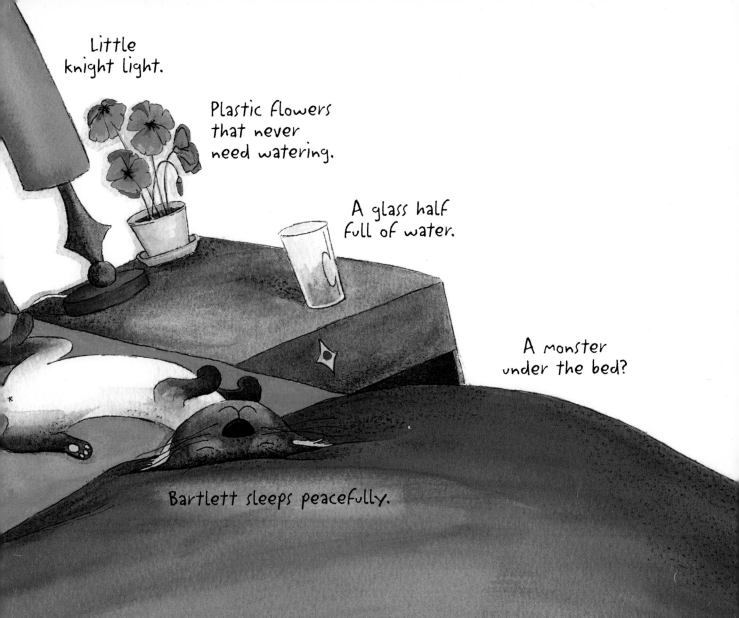

Little knight light.

Plastic flowers that never need watering.

A glass half full of water.

A monster under the bed?

Bartlett sleeps peacefully.

Once upon a time there was a little knight who never fought any battles, because there were no enemies around. He spent long days reading and planting flowers, long nights dreaming and snoring.

But one morning: BANG! BANG! BANG! Someone was knocking on the fortress door, yelling, "HELP! HELP!"

The little knight's hair stands on end.

Two cats run away. They do not like mushrooms.

Mr. and Mrs. Singer shake all over.

A little mushroom that fell from the basket.

Basket for mushrooms picked in the forest.

Book about mushrooms.

The little knight woke with a start. He went downstairs, opened the fortress door and saw his neighbours.

"Help us, help us! Our triplets have been captured by the forest monsters!" cried Mrs. Singer.

"The ogre has the first, the witch has the second and the ghost has the third!" said Mr. Singer, trembling.

The little knight did not hesitate. "Hang on, I'll be right back!" he answered.

Tiny sword, completely harmless but very pretty.

Bartlett does not wear armour.

Quickly, the little knight ran through all the rooms in his fortress to find his equipment.

He found: his sword in the sink ... his breastplate on the television ... his red cape in the bathroom.

Breastplate on top of the television.

A clean cape beside the toilet.

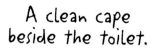

Pointy boots, quite
new, which make his
feet hurt a bit.

He found his boots behind a door ... his gloves
under the toboggan.

Finally dressed in all his armour, the little knight
drank a large glass of milk and devoured a huge
piece of chocolate cake.

Red cape ...
because the
blue one is in
the wash.

The crows are
flying away.

The little knight jumped on his horse and told
the Singers: "Take refuge in my fortress. I will
go to meet my destiny!"

He galloped down the mountain, crossed foggy
fields and was soon in the middle of the deep,
dark forest. The trees moaned in the wind and
shadows reached out like serpents.

Suddenly his horse began to tremble. In the
distance lay the ogre's lair.

Frightful
carnivorous plants.

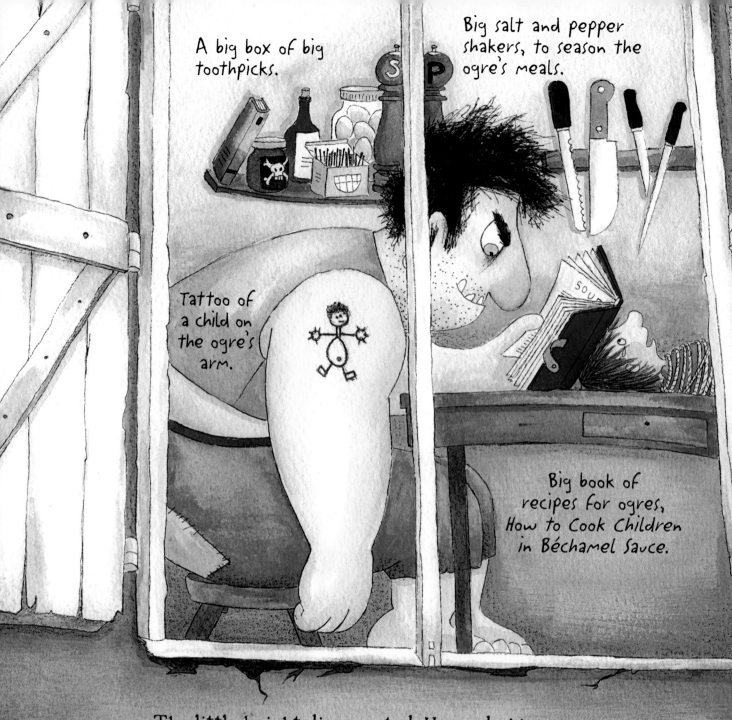

A big box of big toothpicks.

Big salt and pepper shakers, to season the ogre's meals.

Tattoo of a child on the ogre's arm.

Big book of recipes for ogres, How to Cook Children in Béchamel Sauce.

The little knight dismounted. He made his way through the trees, approached the cabin and looked in the window. The ogre was reading a cookbook with a smile on his face. The smallest of the triplets lay bound on the table.

Without wasting a second, the little knight
threw himself into the ogre's house. Caught
off guard, the monster had no time to react.
In two moments, three moves, the little knight
had him trussed like a turkey.

At full gallop, the little knight returned the first triplet to his parents. He inhaled a huge piece of chocolate cake, then returned to the heart of the forest. All of a sudden the horse, frightened, stopped once more. The witch's house appeared in the distance.

The little knight got off his horse and approached the house. He looked in the window. The witch was piling logs to build a fire. The second triplet was tied up, in a cauldron.

The witch flees the scene of the crime.

A toad is hiding in the hay.

Blacky, the witch's cat, hates smoke.

The second triplet loves the little knight.

Bartlett runs away.

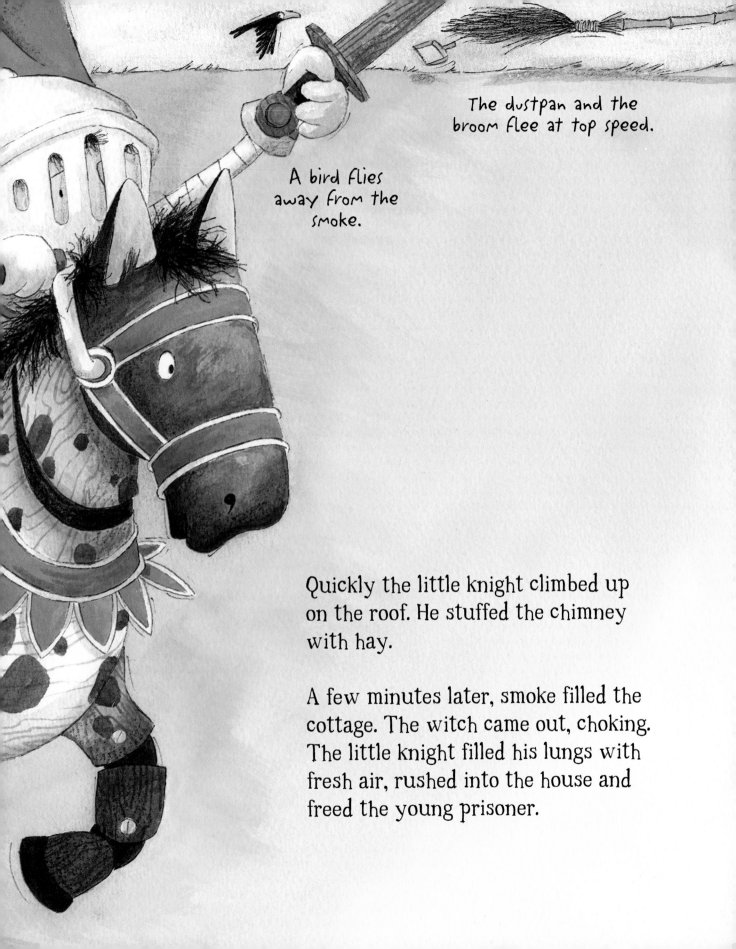

The dustpan and the broom flee at top speed.

A bird flies away from the smoke.

Quickly the little knight climbed up on the roof. He stuffed the chimney with hay.

A few minutes later, smoke filled the cottage. The witch came out, choking. The little knight filled his lungs with fresh air, rushed into the house and freed the young prisoner.

The little knight stays calm, despite the dire situation.

At the speed of light, the little knight brought the second triplet to his parents. He wolfed down another even more enormous piece of chocolate cake, then dove back even deeper into the forest. Suddenly, his horse whinnied in fright. Near an abandoned castle, a ghost appeared in the air. The largest of the triplets was bound to a tree.

The little knight looked the ghost right in the eye. In a soft, calm voice, he whispered some strange words: "Mmm ... Mmm ... Mmm ... Megniiim, megnaaam, megnooom, megnuuum ..."

The ghost, not understanding, came closer and closer. When he was very close, the little knight yelled in his ear, "YAAAAAAAHHHHH!!!"

A crow on top of the himney.

Two birds watch and place bets.

The ghost doesn't look very nice.

Book of ghost jokes.

The third triplet's teeth are chattering. He's never seen a real ghost before.

Bartlett is hiding somewhere.

Frightened by the little knight's ferocious cry, the ghost fled deeper into the forest. The little knight freed the largest of the triplets. Once untied, he ran straight toward the village.

Happy to have succeeded in his mission, the little knight took a break. He picked some flowers, spoke to the birds, whistled a tune. But suddenly the ground shook beneath his feet. BOOM! BOOM! BOOM! The ogre, the witch and the ghost were coming toward him.

"I will haunt your nightmares," said the ghost.
"I'll eat you up," said the ogre.
"I'll turn you into a pumpkin," added the witch.

The ghost's eyes look angry.

The ogre has a long scar.

The ogre's eyes look very, very angry.

A frightened bird flies away upside down.

The witch's eyes look very, very, very angry.

The witch's nails are very sharp.

The little knight planted his sword in the ground.
He took off his armour, lay down on the grass
and said, "Go ahead, eat me up! Turn me into
a pumpkin! Haunt my nightmares! You are the
strongest, the meanest, the scariest!"

Surprised, the monsters leaned over the little
knight and asked: "But . . . but aren't you scared?
Aren't you shaking with fear? Don't you want to
run away?"

"No! I LIKE YOU!" said the little knight, smiling and
reaching out his arms.

The groundhog is
not happy.

The sword is in
the groundhog's
burrow.

Where is
Bartlett?

Shock shows on the ghost's face.

Astonishment shows on the ogre's face.

Surprise shows on the witch's face.

A warm smile on the little knight's face.

The end of a little branch pokes the little knight in the back.

The monsters, stunned by the little knight's words, said, "What? Say that again?"

The little knight got up. He made up a little dance and began to sing: "I like you! I liike you! I liiiiiiike you! I like yooooou!"

There is kindness in the ghost's eyes.

There is gentleness on the witch's face.

Hares watch in astonishment.

The little knight's made-up dance.

Bartlett can't believe her eyes.

There is goodness in the ogre's eyes.

The monsters stared in astonishment.

"That's the first time anyone has ever liked me," said the witch.

Birds watch in astonishment.

"Me too," said the ogre.

"And me," said the ghost.

Foxes watch in astonishment.

"That's nice! MORE, MORE!" said the monsters.

While the little knight danced and spun, singing his friendly song, the witch said to the ogre, "Did you know you have beautiful eyes?"

Then they took turns complimenting each other:

"You have lovely teeth!"

"You have a beautiful smile!"

"You have strong legs!"

Two birds compliment each other.

Fabulous hair.

A lovely voice comes from the witch's mouth.

Two flowers compliment each other.

Strong legs.

Two turtles make up a dance.

"You have a cute chin!"

"You have fabulous hair!"

"You have nice hands!"

"You have a lovely voice!"

"You have pretty feet!"

"You have perfect ears!"

After singing and dancing with his new friends, the little knight put his armour back on, climbed on his horse and asked the monsters: "Do you want more kindness and affection?"

"Yes, yes, YEEESSSS!" they chorused.

"Then come with me!" said the little knight.

The ogre, the witch and the ghost followed the little knight. Singing, they left the deep, dark forest and climbed the big hill that led to the fortress.

The villagers ar a bit nervous at first but after few minutes it's okay . . .

Attracted by the singing, the villagers came to look at the monsters. Smiling, the ogre, witch and ghost emptied their pockets and gave gifts to everyone.

George forester gets a pretty pebble as a gift.

Bartlett and Blacky are friends for life.

Chocolate cake crumbs.

The little knight lit a big bonfire. They sang.
They made up dances. They ate HUGE pieces
of chocolate cake.

At midnight, the parents wanted to put their
kids to bed, but they all refused to go . . .

The bonfire lights
up the night.

Mr. Baxter gets a
mushroom as a gift.

Happy smile.

So to help the children get to sleep, the little knight asked the monsters to sing them sweet lullabies — as sweet as chocolate!